The Perfect Day

The Perfect Day
A Picture Corgi Book 0 552 525138
Originally published in Great Britain by The Bodley Head Ltd

PRINTING HISTORY
The Bodley Head edition published 1986
Picture Corgi edition published 1989

Picture Corgi Books are published by Transworld Publishers Ltd., 61-63 Uxbridge Road, Ealing, London W5 5SA, in Australia by Transworld Publishers (Australia) Pty. Ltd., 15-23 Helles Avenue, Moorebank, NSW 2170, and in New Zealand by Transworld Publishers (N.Z.) Ltd., Cnr. Moselle and Waipareira Avenues, Henderson, Auckland.
Made and Printed in Portugal by Printer Portuguesa

For Max

The Perfect Day

John Prater

Picture Corgi Books

The Smiths are off to the seaside for the day.

Soon everything is packed up, and everyone is ready to go.

Everyone, that is, except Kevin.

But at last they are on their way.

The sun shines and the birds sing.

They can't wait to get down to the beach.

It's a beautiful day, and there are lots of interesting places to explore.

The sea is warm and calm.

At lunchtime they eat at a lovely
open-air restaurant.

It's not fair!   I've only
got one straw. I always
have two straws at home.

In the afternoon they go to the zoo,
and arrive just in time to see the seals
being fed.

oh-_ee_!

Then they go to the funfair on the sea-front.

Kevin and his sister have a go on nearly everything

and they both win a prize.

But at the end of a perfect day, a sudden storm sends the family rushing for their car.

**Here are some other Picture Corgis you
may enjoy:-**

A KISS ON THE NOSE

by Tony Bradman; illustrated by Sumiko

TEDDY TRUCKS

by Michelle Cartlidge

KIT AND THE MAGIC KITE

by Helen Cooper

GILBERT'S GOBSTOPPER

by Mark Haddon

LUCY AND TOM AT THE SEASIDE

by Shirley Hughes

WINSTON'S ICE CREAM CAPER

by Andrew Martyr and Paula Lawford

WHAT-A-MESS AT THE SEASIDE

by Frank Muir; illustrated by Joseph Wright

MY HOLIDAY

by Sumiko